Dear Parent:
Your child's love of reading starts here!

Every child learns to read in a different way and at his or her own speed. Some go back and forth between reading levels and read favorite books again and again. Others read through each level in order. You can help your young reader improve and become more confident by encouraging his or her own interests and abilities. From books your child reads with you to the first books he or she reads alone, there are I Can Read Books for every stage of reading:

SHARED READING
Basic language, word repetition, and whimsical illustrations, ideal for sharing with your emergent reader

BEGINNING READING
Short sentences, familiar words, and simple concepts for children eager to read on their own

READING WITH HELP
Engaging stories, longer sentences, and language play for developing readers

READING ALONE
Complex plots, challenging vocabulary, and high-interest topics for the independent reader

I Can Read Books have introduced children to the joy of reading since 1957. Featuring award-winning authors and illustrators and a fabulous cast of beloved characters, I Can Read Books set the standard for beginning readers.

A lifetime of discovery begins with the magical words "I Can Read!"

Visit www.icanread.com for information
on enriching your child's reading experience.

I Can Read® and I Can Read Book® are trademarks of HarperCollins Publishers.

Danny and the Dinosaur in the Big City
Copyright © 2019 by The Authors Guild Foundation, Anti-Defamation League Foundation, ORT America, Inc., United Negro College Fund, Inc.
www.icanread.com

Library of Congress Control Number: 2018960509
ISBN 978-0-06-241060-3 (trade bdg.)—ISBN 978-0-06-241059-7 (pbk.)

19 20 21 22 23 SCP 10 9 8 7 6 5 4 3 2 1 ❖ First Edition

Syd Hoff's

DANNY AND THE DINOSAUR

in the Big City

by Bruce Hale

pictures in the style of Syd Hoff

by Charles Grosvenor and David A. Cutting

HARPER

An Imprint of HarperCollinsPublishers

"Guess where we're going?"

Danny asked his friend the dinosaur.

"Where?" asked the dinosaur.

4

"My class is taking a field trip
in the big city," said Danny.
"And you're invited too!"

5

The next day, Danny and his class
rode in a yellow bus.
The dinosaur had to walk,
but he didn't mind.

The view was amazing!

Everyone stared at the city.

Such tall skyscrapers!

So many people!

So much traffic!

Danny's class went to a big park.
Everyone rode the carousel
except the dinosaur.

"Sorry, you're too big,"
said the carousel operator.

When Danny and his class

rode the fireboat,

Danny even got to sound the siren!

The dinosaur couldn't fit,

so he swam beside the boat.

13

The class visited
a fancy music hall.

Everybody loved watching

the famous dancers do their dance.

Kick, kick, kick!

But when the dinosaur
joined the dancers,
everything shook!

To reach the subway,

Danny's class rode the escalator.

The dinosaur didn't know

what to make of moving stairs!

But everyone was excited
to ride underground.

When Danny's class
visited the big square,
the dinosaur was a real hit.

"Nice costume, buddy!"

shouted a construction worker.

Then the class walked along
the old railroad line,
where they could see the whole city
spread out below them.

In late afternoon,
Danny's class went
to see Lady Liberty.
Everyone was amazed.

"The statue is so big!" said Danny.

"It's just the right size,"

said the dinosaur.

"I've never felt small before!"

As the sun sank low,

it was time to leave.

Danny's class sang songs

all the way back home.

The dinosaur helped.

When at last they got home,

Danny and the dinosaur said,

"Where will we go

on our next field trip?"